The Spotlight Club Mysteries

•

A SPOTLIGHT CLUB MYSTERY

Mystery of the Midnight Message

Florence Parry Heide and Roxanne Heide

Illustrations by Seymour Fleishman

ALBERT WHITMAN & Company, Chicago

Library of Congress Cataloging in Publication Data

Heide, Florence Parry.
  Mystery of the midnight message.

  (A Spotlight Club mystery) (Pilot books)
  SUMMARY: While stranded in a half-empty motel during
a blizzard, the Spotlight Club detectives receive a
mysterious phone call about a crime in the making.
  [1. Mystery and detective stories] I. Heide,
Roxanne, joint author. II. Fleishman, Seymour.
III. Title.
PZ7.H36Myg   [Fic]   77-14382
ISBN 0-8075-5381-6

Text © 1977 by Florence Parry Heide and Roxanne Heide
Illustrations © 1977 by Albert Whitman & Company
Published simutaneously in Canada by
George J. McLeod, Limited, Toronto
All rights reserved. Printed in U.S.A.

Contents

Mystery of the
Midnight Message

1 · Snowbound

THE BUS SKIDDED on the snow and swerved around a corner. Cindy and Jay Temple pressed their faces against the darkened window and peered out.

"What a snowstorm!" exclaimed Cindy. Huge snowflakes loomed up to the window, leaving wet tracks as they melted.

"We'll never get home at this rate," complained Jay.

"Well, it was worth it, going to John's for his birthday party. I loved seeing all our cousins again."

The bus slowed to a snail's pace. The bus driver

spoke over his shoulder in a loud firm voice. "It looks as though we're going to have to slow down a bit because of the weather, folks, but the bus and I are doing the best we can. By the way, my name's Luke." He leaned forward and shook his head. "Pretty bad night."

Jay groaned. "If we slow down any more we'll be going backwards," he whispered to Cindy.

The bus skidded again, pushing Cindy against Jay. "I can hardly see the other side of the road," she said. She glanced up to the driver's seat and saw swirls of snow beating against the front window. Luke sat hunched forward, leaning over the steering wheel.

The bus slowed even more and came to a stop. Luke stood up and faced the passengers. "Looks like we've got ourselves a problem, folks," he announced. "The windshield wiper just can't move fast enough to clear the snow off." He shook his head and pressed his lips together. The passengers looked expectantly at him.

Luke cleared his throat. "It so happens there's a little motel, just where I've stopped the bus. That's pretty lucky, folks. Because we're going to have to spend the night here."

Sounds of excitement filled the bus. Cindy hurriedly began checking her purse. "We won't possibly have enough money to spend the night at a motel," she whispered. "We'll have to sleep here on the bus."

"And of course," Luke went on, "the bus company will take care of all expenses, including breakfast. Sorry about the inconvenience, folks, but it's just one of those things."

Voices filled the bus. People stood up to reach for their coats.

"Whoa, hold on there a second," Luke said cheerfully. "I've got to check out the motel, make sure there's room for us. Can't tell a thing about it from the outside. Just stay inside the bus until I talk to the desk clerk about our problem. It will confuse things if we all rush in at once."

The passengers sat down again, talking loudly with each other. "An adventure," whispered Cindy.

As Luke opened the door, blankets of snow blew inside the warm bus. He threw his scarf around his face and hurriedly stepped out.

"Dexter's going to be sorry he wasn't with us," said Jay. Dexter Tate, their next-door neighbor, was the third detective in their Spotlight Club.

"Mom was expecting us home at nine o'clock, and it's almost that now," worried Cindy, glancing at her watch. "And we're barely halfway home. Let's call her as soon as we get inside the motel."

In a few moments Luke burst back through the door. He was covered with snow. "We're all in luck, folks. It's warm and cozy inside, there's plenty of room for everybody, and the desk clerk said that if any of you were hungry the kitchen would be open for another half hour."

"Whew," said Jay in relief. "I've been thinking 'food' for three hours."

The passengers got up from their seats again and headed for the door. Huge snowflakes slapped Jay's and Cindy's faces as they hurried down the bus steps and into the blizzard. Warm lights inside the motel looked blurry and faded through the thick mask of snow.

"Hurry up, folks," called Luke from the entrance of the motel. "It's cold out there."

In a moment all the passengers had filed into the motel. Jay took his place in line at the desk.

"There's a phone," said Cindy, pointing to a pay phone right across from the clerk. "I'll hurry and tell Mom what's happened while you get us a room."

By the time Cindy had finished her phone call, Jay was the only one left in line.

"Now what did I do with—" the desk clerk was saying, looking anxiously around him. His hair was sticking out over his glasses, which were tilted. "I— ah—here we are," he said, pulling out a new sheaf of registration forms.

He took a deep breath and sighed. "Wouldn't you know, my second night on the job and something like this has to happen. A whole busload of people to register, all these forms to fill out and file, and I haven't even had time to eat my sandwich. Plus, my car probably won't start in this weather in the morning." He shook his head. "I don't mean to bother you with all my problems, but I'm new here. And, frankly, I was reaching the screaming point. My name's Chick, by the way."

Jay and Cindy introduced themselves. "Do I just sign our names?" asked Jay.

Chick nodded. He peered through his glasses at a form in front of him. "And put down where you're from. You came on that bus, so we can skip all the other stuff."

Jay wrote down the information and pushed the form back across the desk.

"Here's your key," said Chick, reaching up behind him into the rows of wooden boxes that held the motel keys. "Number 210. I'm not sure which corridor it's on, I'm too new here. It's on this floor, I know that much. All the rooms are here because there isn't any other floor."

He handed the key to Jay. "The motel coffee shop is down that way," he said, pointing. "If you're hungry, I suggest you hurry. They'll be closing in a few minutes."

"Let's hurry," urged Jay.

Chick sighed. "I've got to be on duty all night. Until my replacement comes in the morning. And in this weather, he may never come." He sighed again and then busied himself with forms at the desk.

Cindy and Jay headed for the coffee shop. "I'm glad I called Mom," said Cindy. "She was just starting to get worried. She'd been listening to the weather reports. She thinks we're having a great adventure, now that she's not worried anymore."

After they had had a hamburger, Jay and Cindy started to look for their room. They walked down the corridor, checking the numbers on the doors. "204, 206, 208, and here we are—210," said Jay, taking the key out of his pocket. They were alone in the hallway which stretched silently beyond them to an exit door.

"Door after door and not a sound anywhere," whispered Cindy. "It's kind of spooky."

Jay opened their door, and they stepped inside. The room was in total darkness. Cindy held back while Jay felt around the wall for the light switch. He flicked it on, and the room was flooded with warm light.

"Hey, look," Jay said. "Our own TV."

"And a telephone," added Cindy. "Right in our own room."

They threw their jackets on one of the beds and

15

began a tour of the room. "Our own bathroom," announced Cindy. "And closets you can walk into."

"And how about this?" asked Jay, opening the desk drawers. "Stationery, postcards, and a pen. Who will we write to?"

"Dexter," suggested Cindy. " 'Having a grand time, wish you were here.' How's that?" She took a sheet of stationery and an envelope from the desk drawer and wrote quickly. Then she handed it to Jay. "I wrote, you mail. That's what's called dividing the chores."

Jay grinned and put the envelope in his pocket. "We can save a stamp. I'll give it to him tomorrow."

Just then there was a knock on the door. Jay opened it. A tall man with dark hair and glasses stood in the corridor. His dark blue suit looked old but neatly pressed. A bright yellow tie hung loosely from his frayed collar.

"Hello! I'm Monty Montague—the name rhymes with clue," he said, smiling.

Cindy smiled back. She thought that he wasn't actually *thin*. His suit was just too large.

"I've brought you toothbrushes and tooth-

paste, special gifts of the Travelers' Toothsome," he went on. He winked behind his glasses and held out a handful of small toothbrushes in plastic bags. "Free samples for one and all. My company will love me for making their toothbrushes popular. Rhymes with rich and famous, which is what I hope to be someday. Did you ever hear of anyone getting rich and famous selling toothbrushes?" He shrugged. "Neither did I."

Cindy and Jay smiled at him.

"Pick a color, any color," Monty said. "Red, white, blue, orange, pink, green—rhymes with clean."

They each chose a toothbrush.

"Remember my name. Monty Montague, rhymes with clue. Here's my card to remind you." He smiled and started walking down the corridor.

"Thanks a lot," called Jay.

"Nice," said Cindy, closing the door. "And, actually, that's all I have the energy for—brushing my teeth."

"And climbing into bed," added Jay. "The long bus ride, the snow, everything just hit me." In a few minutes he said, "Cindy? Did you remember to put the chain back on the door after Monty left?"

There was no answer.

"Are you asleep already?" asked Jay.

"Mmmph," said Cindy.

Jay turned over, pulling the crisp sheets up to his chin. He yawned and turned over again. Suddenly he tensed and lay motionless. A key was turning in the locked door. And then the door slowly started to open.

2 · Midnight Message

JAY JUMPED instantly out of bed. "Cindy," he whispered urgently, keeping his eyes on the slowly opening door.

Cindy sat up in bed. She gasped. A tall shadow loomed in the doorway, outlined by the dim light from the corridor. The man stood in silence for a moment, then his long arm reached for the switch on the wall.

Suddenly the room was light. Cindy and Jay blinked. It was Luke.

He took a step backwards in surprise. "What are you kids doing in here?" he asked, frowning.

"Oh, it's you," breathed Jay in relief. "We were scared for a minute."

"Not me," said Cindy. "I was too sleepy to be scared."

Luke looked down at the key in his hand. "This is 210, isn't it?" he asked. They nodded. "I was supposed to stay in here. The desk clerk must have got mixed up. He gave you my room."

He looked around. "Guess I'd better check it out with him and see where I should sleep tonight. Sorry to have bothered you. Go back to sleep." He turned the switch on the wall again, and the room was plunged into darkness. "We'll be on our way in the morning," he announced. "The snow is stopping."

He shut the door.

Cindy sighed and pulled the covers up again.

"Chick must really be mixed up," said Cindy. "Giving the key to this room to someone else when we were in it. That's not supposed to happen."

"Maybe he's just sleepy," said Jay. "I would be if I had to work all night."

"Nothing is going to get me awake now," vowed Cindy, turning over.

They were both sound asleep in a moment.

A sudden shrill ring wakened Jay. He reached out to shut off the alarm. No, it wasn't an alarm. Where was he, anyway? What time was it? He looked at his watch. It was a few minutes after twelve.

Snowstorm. Motel. But what was ringing?

The telephone. He stumbled across the room in the dark to answer. A woman's voice spoke. "Just listen. Don't talk." Her voice was low and without expression.

"Your half is there. Desk drawer. Leave in the morning. It's only a hundred miles, but the roads are bad."

Jay took a breath, ready to interrupt. "Don't talk," the voice repeated. "You must be there by eight sharp. The house will be empty. Bee will meet you with his half. You'll have one hour, not more, at the house. By the way, the last problem has been taken care of. The dog Tarrawig has been poisoned."

Jay's heart pounded. What was going on? A dog poisoned?

The woman's low flat voice continued. "This will be our last contact until afterwards."

The phone went dead.

"Who was it?" Cindy asked sleepily. She sat up in bed and turned on the light.

Quickly Jay told Cindy about the telephone call. "And a dog named Tarrawig has been poisoned."

Cindy gasped and reached for her notebook. "Don't forget anything," she urged. "Not until I've written it all down."

"How could I forget anything like this?" asked Jay.

"You're positive you didn't dream it?" asked Cindy.

"Don't be silly," said Jay. He frowned. "Bee is going to be at the house with his half," he repeated slowly.

Cindy wrote:

> *Query*: Who is Bee?
>
> What house?
>
> Half of what?

"The woman said, 'Your half is there in the desk drawer.' But the drawers are empty." Jay

opened and closed them again. "Nothing but that stationery."

"Half of what, I wonder?" asked Cindy.

"Maybe half of some stolen loot," suggested Jay.

Cindy walked over to the desk. "Well, whatever it was isn't here now," she said. "Or maybe it was a wrong number. You're sure she said half was in the desk?"

Jay shut his eyes, trying to remember.

"Maybe she said behind the desk," said Cindy. "Let's—"

"Wait a minute," said Jay, frowning. "I'm trying to concentrate." Suddenly he snapped his fingers. "She said, 'Your half is there.' Then she said, 'Desk drawer.' Not 'in'. Just 'desk drawer.' "

Quickly he started to lift out the stationery drawer. He turned it upside down to examine it. "Nothing. No false panel, no nothing."

"Try the others," urged Cindy.

Jay lifted out another drawer and started to turn it over. They stared. A white envelope was taped to the back of the drawer.

Jay frowned at the envelope. Then he felt it. "Feels like a key of some kind," he said.

"Open it," urged Cindy. "There's something bad going on. It's our business to find out what it is."

Jay opened the envelope carefully. "It is a key," breathed Cindy.

"And something else," said Jay, opening a piece of paper. Cindy looked over his shoulder. This is what they saw.

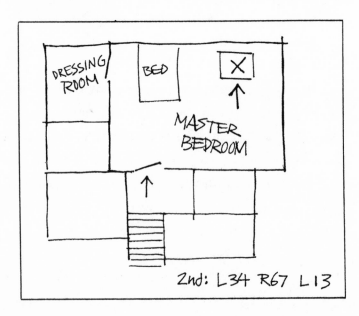

Cindy peered closer. "It's a diagram of a house. It shows bedrooms. And it's the second floor."

"And what's the code?" wondered Jay. "It must be directions," he decided. "Like a map in a treasure hunt, something like that. Turn left for thirty-four feet, then right for sixty-seven feet, and so on. Until the treasure."

"And then there must be a keyhole, and this . . . is the key," added Cindy.

Jay looked again at the mysterious code. "L," he muttered. "R." Suddenly he stopped and stared. "Gym class!" he exclaimed excitedly.

Cindy raised her eyebrows. "What?"

"We were all given slips of paper with the combination to our own locker," said Jay. "That's what this is—a combination!"

"To a gym locker?" asked Cindy.

They stared at each other. "To a safe," she whispered.

She leaned over the diagram. "Look," she said in a moment. "Here is the master bedroom. There's an arrow. Pointing to an *X*. The *X* is the safe!"

She took a deep breath.

Jay rubbed his forehead. "And someone's going to open that safe. With this combination. And rob it."

"Tomorrow night," said Cindy. "Tonight, really. It's already after midnight."

"We've got to stop them," announced Jay firmly. "But there's no address, no name."

"It's like looking for a needle in a haystack," added Cindy, shaking her head.

She opened her notebook and copied down the code. "Second," she muttered. She flipped a page and studied her notes. "Look," she said. "The woman said 'your half.' Not half of some loot or something—half of the combination."

"And Bee has the other half, " Jay broke in. "The first half. Because this note says *second*. Second half of the combination."

"What about the key?" asked Cindy. "It isn't half a key."

"No, but maybe there's another key," said Jay. "Bee has half the combination, and he has the other key."

"Two keys," mused Cindy.

"One to one door and one to another," suggested Jay.

Cindy nodded excitedly. "The woman who called has left one key and one half of the combination with whoever was supposed to be in Room 210, and the other key and the other half of the combination with Bee. That way neither of them can open the safe alone."

Jay looked at Cindy's notebook.

"It's not like looking for a needle in a haystack after all," he said in a moment. "All we need to do is to find out who was supposed to be in this room. And—" He paused, frowning. "Luke came here tonight, remember? And he had a key to 210."

"But that was Chick's fault," Cindy protested.

"Or was it?" asked Jay. "After all, it was Luke who decided the bus should stop here tonight. If it hadn't been snowing his excuse could have been that there was something wrong with the bus."

"Monty Montague came here tonight, too," Cindy said slowly. "But—"

She jumped up. "Let's find out from Chick. Let's see if anyone had reserved this room for tonight. It will be in the records. Was it really Luke?"

"Let's go," said Jay, slipping on his shoes. "Lucky we're sleeping half-dressed."

They opened the door carefully and stood listening.

3 · Clues in the Records

THE LONG CORRIDOR was silent and dimly lighted. Cindy and Jay tiptoed down the empty halls until they came to the lobby. Chick was sitting hunched up, reading a notebook.

"Hi, Chick," said Jay, walking up to the desk.

Chick jumped and turned around, his eyes wide behind his glasses.

"Oh, it's you," he said, relieved. "I thought—"

31

He took off his glasses and rubbed his face. "I thought everyone would be asleep by now. That telephone call got you awake, huh?"

Jay glanced quickly at Cindy. Had Chick listened in? Was he in on the robbery?

"All calls go through the switchboard," said Chick. "That's how I know about it." He swallowed and cleared his throat.

Jay spoke firmly. "The call wasn't for us. It was for whoever was supposed to be in Room 210. We want to find out who it was and how we can reach him. That way we can give him the message."

Chick stared at them blankly.

"You'll have the reservation there in your records," suggested Cindy.

"My records," said Chick vaguely. He scratched his chin. "Well, maybe someone had reserved that room. I don't remember. I don't remember anything right now," he confessed. "I'm not used to staying up all night."

"Just check to see if someone else was supposed to have that room tonight," urged Cindy. "210."

Chick sighed and took out a big ledger. He looked through it. Then he leafed through some cards.

Cindy's heart pounded. What if they found out that Luke had reserved the room? That would mean he'd known ahead of time that the bus would stop here. That would mean—

"Here it is," said Chick finally. "Room 210. I remember now. Mr. A. Scull from Cleveland called. He asked for that particular room. 210. Told me not to let anybody else take it. But he never showed up. And then when all of you came in, I got mixed up and assigned the room to you."

Cindy made a mental note of the name. A. Scull. Cleveland, Ohio. But of course a person could make up any name. Even Luke could have reserved that room under another name to make sure it would be empty.

"Maybe this Scull was caught in the snow-storm," said Chick. "Probably stayed somewhere else. Never bothered to cancel. People should cancel, you know. It's very inconsiderate."

He pursed his lips. "If you'll just leave the message here with me—the message that you say someone telephoned in for him—I'll see that he gets it. That is, if he ever comes. He probably will never show up."

He'll show up, thought Cindy. If there is a Mr.

Scull, he'll come for the key and the combination. She shivered and glanced behind her down the long dim corridor.

Jay spoke quickly. "Chick, who had the room before we did?" Cindy glanced at Jay. Of course. Whoever was there before had hidden the envelope.

Chick took out a handkerchief and blew his nose. "Before you? Oh, you mean the message was for them, maybe?" He leafed through his records. Jay and Cindy looked at each other, holding their breath. Maybe they could find out enough to put this puzzle together. Before it was too late.

Chick held up a card. "Jane E. Jones, Chicago. Took the room yesterday, but the maid said she didn't spend the night. Never even used a towel. Just checked in and out."

A woman. The woman on the phone. Jay took a deep breath. "What did she look like?" he asked.

"Never saw her," said Chick, shaking his head. "I wasn't here when she checked in, and I didn't see her when she left. She'd paid in advance for the room, so of course she was free to leave when she liked."

He shrugged his thin shoulders. "Imagine, paying for a motel room and then never even using it. Some people must have a lot of money to waste."

Cindy and Jay exchanged glances. Jane Jones. A. Scull. Who were they? What were their real names? Who else was in the gang? Luke? Monty? What would they do when they found out that Jay and Cindy had the key and half the combination?

"Thanks, Chick," said Jay. He and Cindy turned to go. Cindy took a deep breath. The corridor seemed even longer and dimmer. She breathed a sigh of relief when they stepped into their room.

"This time let's be sure to put the chain on the door," she said. "And let's put a chair in front of the door, wedged under the doorknob. And—"

"And a bucket of water to fall on Scull's head when he walks in," laughed Jay.

"It isn't funny," said Cindy. "It's dangerous. He was supposed to get that message. Scull and Bee can't rob the safe without this part of the combination. When Scull and Jane Jones find out that we got the message and that we found the key and the combination—" She paused, frowning.

"Jane Jones won't try to call him again because she thinks she's already talked to him," said Jay. "And she said this would be their last contact until afterwards."

"But when he doesn't hear from her, he'll try to call her," said Cindy positively. "He'll find out the combination some way. And they'll rob that safe tonight. We've got to keep them from getting there first."

"All we know is that the house is a hundred miles from here," said Jay.

"Well, that's not much, but it's something," answered Cindy.

She studied her notes again. "Tarrawig," she said. "That's an unusual name. Maybe it's an unusual dog. Was an unusual dog, I mean," she added, blinking. "Maybe we could find something out at the library when we get home."

Jay shook his head. "We'll be too late."

"Never give up. That should be the Spotlight Club motto." She wrote it down. "There. Possible Motto: 'Never Give Up'. Let's take a vote when we see Dexter."

"We've got to get some sleep tonight," said Jay.

"I'm not a bit sleepy now," said Cindy. "Mysteries really keep me wide awake."

"Would you rather sleep with the light on?" asked Jay.

"Of course not," insisted Cindy. "The chair under the door will be enough."

They lay in bed talking, their eyes wide open, their thoughts racing. Jane Jones had called to deliver the message to A. Scull. Scull and another person, Bee, were going to rob a safe. Each was supposed to have half the combination. Each was supposed to have a key. Now Jay and Cindy had Scull's key and Scull's half of the combination.

Where was the house? How could they find out in time?

They tossed and turned all night.

Cindy opened her eyes and sat up in bed. It was morning. Someone was tapping lightly at the door. A key turned in the lock. Was it Scull?

Cindy reached over to Jay's bed and shook him.

The key turned a second time. Someone tried to

push open the door, again and again. "Jay," whispered Cindy urgently.

Jay jumped awake. They stared at the door.

It must be Scull.

Jay got out of bed and walked over to the barricaded door. He held his breath.

4 · Who's to Be Trusted?

"DON'T YOU DARE open that door," whispered Cindy urgently. "He can't get in, not with that chain and that chair. He won't try to knock the door down, either. This is a motel. We're not all alone. Someone would hear."

They stared at the doorknob. It turned and turned. The door was pushed against the chair.

"Anybody in there?" called a high, thin voice.

"It's me, the cleaning person, doing my rounds."

Jay sighed in relief. He released the chain and moved the chair away. A spindly young woman stood in the doorway. A scarf was tied around her head, exposing tight brown curls. She wore blue jeans and a faded loose shirt. At her side was a large cart filled with towels and sheets and cleaning supplies.

"Thought all these rooms were empty by now, what with the bus going off pretty soon," she said. "You ready to check out? Because I'm ready to clean your room."

"Not yet," said Jay quickly. "Can you come back later?"

"Guess I'll have to," sighed the thin woman. She peered behind Jay and Cindy into the room. "I suppose I'll have to do all the rooms at once, in one gulp." She sighed and pushed her cart along the corridor, stopping to knock at another door.

Jay frowned. "Maybe she's not really a cleaning person," he said. "Maybe she's a member of the gang. Maybe she just wanted to come in here to look for the envelope. Maybe—"

Cindy laughed. "Maybe we'll be seeing ghosts in the closet next. At this rate, we'll be suspecting each other."

"Well, in a mystery we have to suspect everybody. Just in case."

Jay brightened. "And we'd better have breakfast now, just in case we don't get near a coffee shop again for a while."

"Good," agreed Cindy, opening the door. She jumped in surprise. Luke was standing right outside, staring at her.

"I was just going by," he said. "I thought you'd be at breakfast by now. I saw the cleaning cart down the hall and—" He peered behind them at the room. "The bus is nearly ready to go. I'd say about another half hour or so. Just wanted to be sure that all my passengers would be on board. Can't leave anyone behind, you know."

"We'll be ready," promised Jay.

Luke stepped inside the room and looked around. "Not much luggage, eh?" he chuckled. "Well, it won't be hard loading up the bus."

He smiled at Jay and Cindy. "Had breakfast

yet?" When they shook their heads, Luke said, "Let's go together."

Luke stood aside, waiting until Jay and Cindy were out in the corridor. Then he walked around the room. "Better be sure you don't leave anything. That often happens. People leave things in motel rooms."

"We don't have anything to leave," said Cindy. "Just our jackets, and we wouldn't forget them, in this weather."

"Right you are," said Luke. He took a last look around the room before he walked out to the corridor and closed the door behind him. The three started toward the coffee shop.

Cindy and Jay exchanged glances. Had Luke been listening at their door? He said he'd thought they had already left for breakfast. Did he want them out of the room so he could look for the envelope?

They walked in silence. When they reached the restaurant, Luke clapped Jay on the shoulder. "I'll be right in," he said. "Have to check that old bus one last time before takeoff." He nodded toward the big picture window. The snow had stopped, but the sky was gray and heavy. Jay and Cindy could see the bus standing in the parking lot outside. The snow had been brushed off. Luke must have gotten up early.

When Luke left, Cindy and Jay sat at the counter. Cindy whispered to Jay, "I wonder if he's really going to check on the bus. Or is he going back to our room? He had a key last night. Maybe he never gave it back to Chick. Maybe—"

"Even if he didn't have a key, he could probably get in," Jay whispered back. "The cleaning person is going to be in and out of all those rooms now, cleaning them. He could get in if—"

Suddenly he stopped and took a deep breath. "Look," he said, "out the window."

Cindy turned around. Luke had put on a jacket and was walking toward the bus. He wasn't in their room after all. Cindy and Jay smiled at each other.

They watched as a figure emerged from an old green car near the bus and called something to Luke. It was Monty Montague, smiling his friendly smile and slapping his hands together in the cold air. He left the engine of his car running and talked to Luke for a moment. Then he got in his car again and drove out of sight.

44

"He didn't say good-bye," said Cindy.

"Well, we hardly know him," said Jay.

"I know, but I felt as if he were a friend," sighed Cindy.

They were finishing their breakfast when they heard a familiar voice. It was Monty, asking for a cup of coffee over the counter. "Mighty glad I had a chance to meet you folks," he said cheerfully, taking a sip of steaming coffee. "Don't forget, if you ever think about toothbrushes, and who doesn't sometimes, think of Travelers' Toothsome."

"We thought you'd gone," said Cindy.

Monty shook his head. "Not yet, but almost. I pulled my car over to the other exit door so I could load up my samples. You've no idea how many samples I carry around. I never know when I'll be at a motel that's suddenly filled with a busload of people stranded in a snowstorm."

Jay glanced at the bus again. Luke was checking the windshield wipers and the headlights. He climbed into the bus and out. Then he started to head back toward the motel.

A shiny new red car had just pulled into the parking lot. A large man emerged, taking long strides in the same direction as Luke. They both disappeared around the corner of the building toward the motel entrance.

Jay sighed. "Everything looks normal."

"I don't even know what normal is, anymore," said Cindy. "Not after last night."

They looked around the coffee shop. Other passengers were standing near the door with their jackets and scarves on.

"Everyone's getting ready to leave," said Jay. "Let's get our jackets." They said good-bye to Monty Montague and headed back to their room. As they passed the lobby, they saw Luke leaning over the desk, talking to Chick. Then the switchboard buzzed and Chick answered the telephone. He handed it to Luke. "It's for you," he said. Luke nodded and picked up the telephone. "Twenty-four," they heard him say. Then he listened, nodded, and hung up.

"What did that mean, twenty-four?" said Jay.

Jay and Cindy hurried to their room. "How would anyone know he was here?" Cindy whispered. "He must be part of the gang. Maybe that was Jane Jones on the telephone. Maybe—"

"And maybe Chick is in on it, too," suggested Jay.

"Oh dear," worried Cindy. "Luke, Scull, Chick—I don't trust anyone. Except Monty. I trust him."

Jay was silent. When they came to their room,

Jay turned the key in the lock and opened the door.

Suddenly there was a shrill ring. Cindy jumped and looked at Jay. "Maybe Jane Jones again," she whispered. "You pick it up."

Jay swallowed and reached for the telephone. He waited a moment. Then he heard Chick's voice. "Long distance call for you, just a sec."

In another moment he heard, "Hello? Hello? I'm still trying to reach Jay Temple, please."

The voice was wonderfully familiar.

"Dex!" shouted Jay. "How did you know where we were?"

"I called your mom this morning. She told me you got to stay at that motel. Free! You lucky guys. Now I wish I'd gone with you to your cousin's instead of with Anne to our cousin's. But wait 'til you see the pictures I took!"

"We've got a new mystery, Dex," said Jay. "We found an envelope. Someone's going to rob a safe but we don't know where. We—"

Dexter groaned. "Now I'm really mad I didn't go with you. Look, this is why I called. We're in Farmington. You're taking the bus back to Kenoska this morning, so you could have the bus let you off there on Highway 34 and Hoff Road. You know— there at the Fillson's Farm where Mom and Dad take us sometimes to ride the horses? Anne and I could meet you, and we could all drive home together. You could tell me all about the mystery. I can't wait."

"Perfect!" said Jay, beaming. "We'll bring the envelope we found. Our bus leaves in a few minutes."

"That means you'll get there about two," Dexter interrupted. "Anne and I checked out the mileage before we called you. We'll call the Fillsons and tell them you're on your way. See you there. Can't wait to hear about the mystery. Be sure Cindy takes notes."

"Doesn't she always?" asked Jay.

The operator interrupted. "Your three minutes are up, sir. Signal when through."

"We're through," Dexter said hastily. "Can't afford any more." He hung up. Jay did too, smiling from ear to ear.

"Good. That was Dex. He's meeting us. Hey, we've got to rush. I'll tell you in the bus. Let's grab our jackets."

"It was sure a fun place to stay," said Cindy, walking over to the closet. "Except for all the scares."

"We didn't even get to watch our own private TV," said Jay.

Cindy slid open the large closet doors. She reached her hand into the dark closet for their jackets.

And suddenly her hand touched someone else's hand. It was large and clammy, and its knuckles were covered with hair.

5 · *The Motel Corridor*

CINDY WAS TOO FROZEN to scream. Someone was standing in the closet, inches from her.

The man stared at her, his mouth drawn down into an ugly grimace, his teeth catching a glint of sun from the window in the room.

And then Cindy whirled around, a scream catching in her throat. The man darted from the closet, his huge frame blocking the door to Cindy's and Jay's escape.

They were trapped.

Jay suddenly recognized the man who had driven into the parking lot in the bright red car. And he knew who the man was. Scull. The man who was supposed to get the midnight message. The man who was supposed to have checked into their motel room last night.

Jay ran to Cindy's side. His eyes searched desperately for another way out of the room. The window? They'd never make it.

He returned his frightened gaze to the large man in front of him.

"I heard what you said on the phone. You have the envelope. Give it to me. Now." Scull's mouth pulled down threateningly at the corners, revealing a puckered scar on his lower lip. He walked toward the Spotlighters, scowling, his eyes already searching their clothes.

Instinctively, Cindy clutched her hand to her pocket where she had put the envelope. Scull's thick black eyebrows raised over his narrowed eyes.

"So the girl's got it, eh?" he snarled.

Suddenly Jay reached into his own pocket and

pulled out the envelope he was going to give to Dexter.

"Here you are, I've got it," he called. As Scull reached for the envelope, Jay quickly threw it across the room, over the beds. "There it is!" he cried, grabbing Cindy's arm as Scull lunged toward the envelope.

Jay threw open the door and pulled Cindy with him. They ran down the corridor without stopping to look behind them. They turned a corner, their hearts pounding. The maid's cart was just ahead. Behind it a door was open. They flung themselves into the room and shut the door.

It was empty. The maid had stripped the beds, and she was nowhere in sight. It looked as if she had gone to get some fresh sheets and towels.

Jay and Cindy stood next to the door, their breath coming in short gasps. Footsteps pounded down the hall. Scull. Had he seen them run into this room? He knew now they had the envelope he wanted. He knew they had tricked him.

Barely moving, Jay pressed his ear against the door. The heavy footsteps moved beyond their hiding spot and then stopped. They moved back, more hurriedly this time, and again stopped.

Scull was right outside their door. They could hear him breathing. Did he guess they were hiding there? Even if he hadn't seen them run into the room, would he see the maid's cart and put two and two together? Jay held his breath, not moving, not even looking at Cindy.

There was the sound of two or three doors opening and closing, the murmur of voices, then an angry curse. The footsteps hurried down the corridor again. Soon there was no sound but Cindy's and Jay's hurried breathing.

Jay quietly stepped back from the door and motioned to Cindy to step farther into the room, away from the door.

"He knows we're somewhere in this building," he whispered cautiously. "He probably knows we're supposed to get on that bus. He'll be waiting. We've got to think of something in a hurry."

He glanced at the stripped beds. The maid would be coming back any minute. Cindy frowned and looked quickly around the room. Scull was looking for them. She could almost feel his anger flooding the motel.

"He'll be waiting for us to get on the bus," said Jay. "He can't do anything to us with all those people. But he'll follow the bus. He'll wait for us to get off. And we're getting off at Fillson's farm." Quickly he told Cindy about Dexter's plan to meet them there.

Cindy shuddered. "If we get off the bus there and Scull is following the bus—"

"We can't get on the bus," said Jay firmly, looking at Cindy. "But we've got to get to Fillson's farm."

"I'm scared," admitted Cindy in a small voice. "I just don't want to see that Scull ever again. I can still feel his eyes right through to my bones."

She circled the small motel room and walked to the window.

"I've got it," she whispered excitedly. Her eyes were fastened on an old, shabby car, its green color faded with years and weather. "That old car—the greenish one with the engine running—that's Monty Montague's. He's probably still having one last cup of coffee. We could sneak into his back seat and hide there."

"He could take us to Fillson's," said Jay. "We could escape Scull!"

They crept to the door and listened. Jay opened the door a crack and peered out. The maid's cart was still there in the corridor right in front of them. There was no one in sight.

"The exit door," whispered Cindy. "It's there at the end of this hall. It opens right where Monty's car is parked. We can make a run for it and get inside as fast as we can."

Jay shook his head. "Scull could be coming around the corner of the corridor," he objected.

"I know," said Cindy in a whisper.

She stood motionless, her thoughts racing. "The cart," she said under her breath. "The cleaning person's cart. Who would notice if she pushed it down the hall?"

Cindy ran into the bathroom and grabbed a face towel. Quickly she tied it around her head. Then she opened the door. She glanced around and quickly pulled the cart inside.

"You hide on that bottom shelf," she said. "I'll cover you up with sheets. You'll look like some laundry."

Jay nodded. "It could work. Let's go."

Jay crawled into the space at the bottom of the cart. Cindy took some clean sheets from the pile and shook them out. She covered Jay. She opened the door. No one in sight.

She quickly started to push the cart down the long corridor to the exit. She darted her eyes to every door, afraid one would suddenly open and show Scull grinning at her masquerade. The wheels on the cart screeched loudly.

Cindy glanced down the corridor at the bright exit sign. It seemed miles away. Scull could be hiding anywhere, ready to leap out. She concentrated on steering the cart straight ahead, trying not to run with it. And finally she reached the exit. She peered around her cautiously.

Somewhere a door banged, and Cindy sucked in her breath. She reached down and pulled the sheets off Jay. "Hurry!" she whispered anxiously, looking over her shoulder toward the noise. Jay scrambled out from the cart. Cindy tugged the towel off her hair.

Jay reached for the exit door. He pushed down on the bar handle and groaned, "It won't open!" Cindy shoved with him. It gave way suddenly, letting a blanket of icy air into the corridor. They squinted at the cars parked outside.

"There," whispered Cindy, pointing to Monty's car. It was several parked cars away.

Cindy glanced over her shoulder. Where was Scull? Was he watching them from a window? She forced herself to look only at the cars that stood between them and Monty's car.

They darted through the door and ran to the first car. They crouched beside it, panting, waiting to hear a shout from Scull. Nothing happened.

"Next car," said Cindy, feeling the icy chill on her coatless arms.

"Let's go," whispered Jay.

The snow crunched beneath them as they scrambled along the ground to the next car. They paused only a second to catch their breath and then dashed to Monty's car. Jay reached up to open the back door. It squeaked and Jay stopped, feeling Cindy shivering beside him. He tried it again. and pulled the door open quickly.

They crawled silently into the heated, empty car. Cindy pulled the door after her, careful not to slam it. She'd pull it tight later.

They crouched on the floor, keeping their heads low. Jay looked around the back seat. There was a heavy blue blanket on top of some boxes with bright labels reading "Travelers' Toothsome." He pulled the blanket from the boxes.

"Stay down on the floor. I'll cover us up with this," he whispered to Cindy who was shivering beside him.

Cindy nodded and scrunched herself as small as she could on the floor of the back seat. Jay pulled the blanket over them. Just in time.

The sound of loud, crunching footsteps on the snow reached them. They held their breath. Had Scull seen them after all?

Cindy closed her eyes and waited as she heard someone pulling open the front door of the car. Cold air swirled over the back seat, and then the door shut again. They felt someone sit down in the front seat, and they heard a radio click on.

A cheerful voice started to sing with the music, and Cindy breathed a sigh of relief.

Jay quickly spoke up. "Monty, please don't turn around. It's us, Jay and Cindy, hiding in the back seat."

"Well, I'll be swiggled and swoggled," chuckled Monty. "What have we got here?"

"This is terribly important to us," said Jay urgently. "We're trying to get away from the motel without anyone seeing us. But we can't just leave. We—"

Cindy spoke up. "Someone has to tell Luke that we won't be getting on the bus." She thought quickly. Monty would never agree to their plan if he thought they were in danger.

"We're taking a correspondence course in being detectives," she said hurriedly. "One of the assignments is to sneak away from someplace without being noticed. The assignment is called 'Escape from Danger.'"

"And this is a perfect time to try it," Jay added

eagerly, catching onto Cindy's plan. "Because we're getting picked up at a farm down the road, anyway. By our best friend and his sister."

"And we thought maybe you could drive us there," Cindy continued. "Then Luke, the bus driver, wouldn't have to bother."

They waited eagerly for Monty's reply. At last he sighed. "Ah, how I envy you kids," he said softly. "Of course I'd be glad to help with your detective course. Just tell me what to do."

The Spotlighters hesitated. Then Jay cleared his throat. "There's another part to our course," he said. "We have to figure out from someone else's car everything we can about them. That assignment is called 'Clues and How to Find Them.' Cindy and I have picked out that red car next to the bus." He paused.

"Yes," added Cindy. "If you could walk around there and tell us everything you see in that car, it would help a lot."

"But I'm not taking the course—you are," objected Monty.

"Well, you see, we've got a problem," Jay said.

"We can't complete that clue part of the course without ruining this escaping part. We've got to have you help us."

"Will you?" Cindy asked eagerly.

There was silence from the front seat. Then Monty said, "Sure. What can I lose? I can tell you're good kids, worth helping. What do I tell the bus driver?"

"Just tell him that our mother was worried about us and came to pick us up," Cindy said.

"Will do," Monty said cheerfully. "And I'll check out that car. The flashy red one, you say?"

"Yes," Jay said. "Thanks, Monty."

They heard him opening the car door and felt a cold gust of wind sweep again over the back seat. Then the door slammed, and Cindy and Jay were alone.

"He's going to help us!" Cindy said happily. "We've tricked Scull double. He'll never find us now." She shifted her legs.

In the warm silence of the car, in a cramped position on the back floor, Jay frowned. What if Monty Montague, that cheerful salesman so willing to help him and Cindy, was in on the gang? The thought spun around in his head. What if he and Cindy were in more danger there in the car than they would have been on the bus? Jay felt a tremor run through his body in spite of the warmth of the car. He nudged Cindy.

"What if we can't trust Monty?" he blurted out. "What if he's going over to Luke or Scull and telling them where we are? What if they're all in on the robbery together?"

Jay felt Cindy stiffen next to him. "I never thought of that," she said in a hoarse whisper. "He couldn't, he wouldn't," she said, half to herself. But Monty could be part of it. He'd been talking with Luke out in the parking lot. He'd come to their room the night before. Just to give away toothbrushes? What if Monty told Scull? What if it wasn't Monty who got back in the car, but Scull himself? Cindy's eyes widened at the thought. Her throat tightened and she shivered.

"What if Scull gets in this car instead of Monty?" asked Jay, reading Cindy's thoughts. He pulled the blanket closer around them.

Suddenly there were heavy footsteps outside the car door. Coming closer, crunching on the frozen snow. Monty had been gone a long time. Was it Monty? Or Scull?

The Spotlighters sucked in their breath as the car door opened, and someone sat down heavily on the front seat.

6 · *Some Detective Work*

JAY HAD TENSED himself, ready to leap out of the car with Cindy if Scull got in. And then Monty's voice said, "Everything's been taken care of, kids." He put his car in gear and slowly began to roll out of the parking lot. "You can sit up as soon as we're out of sight."

Jay and Cindy began to unscramble their cramped legs.

"Okay, the coast's clear," Monty said with a chuckle.

Jay and Cindy sat up in the back seat and looked out the window. The motel was slowly getting farther behind them. They breathed a sigh of relief and turned around to face Monty.

"I told the bus driver that your folks had picked you up," said Monty. "He didn't seem too happy about it, I must say," Monty went on.

And no wonder, Cindy thought. If he is in it with Scull, he wouldn't be a bit happy.

"What about the car?" Jay asked. "The red car."

"Oh, yes," Monty said, turning the radio down. "Didn't seem to be too much in there."

"No matter how unimportant it seems to you, it might be very important to us," said Cindy urgently. "For our assignment."

Monty shrugged. "Okay. As far as clues are concerned, here's what I saw. Ready?" He watched them nod in the rear-view mirror. Cindy took out her notebook.

"Front seat: One pair of men's black gloves, one pair of dark glasses," said Monty. "One map, folded over to show Woodvale, which was carefully circled in red pencil."

"Woodvale," repeated Jay. So that's where Scull was headed. "That's not far from Kenoska, Cindy."

Cindy nodded.

"About a hundred miles from here," said Monty. "Not far away in distance, but a million miles away in other respects. I guess almost anyone living in Woodvale must be a millionaire. Big mansions. Huge green lawns." He corrected himself. "Not green. White, this time of year. Snow, you know. Enormous cars, enormous trees, and I expect enormous taxes. It's not for the likes of you and me, a place like Woodvale."

Cindy nudged Jay. Someone in Woodvale was going to be robbed tonight. One of those enormous houses had a safe. An unsafe safe, unless the Spotlighters could do something about the situation before it was too late.

"Anything else?" asked Cindy, her pencil poised.

"Well, let's see," Monty said, swerving the car

gently to avoid a drift in the road. "As I say, Wood-vale was circled in red. In black was the most round-about way of getting there from here that you could dream of. But that's where the car is going, I guess. The markings were from this area where the motel is, right to Woodvale."

Cindy and Jay exchanged glances. Woodvale. At least they'd found out where Scull was going to meet Bee. That was something. But whose house? How could they find out?

Monty kept talking. "A black wool scarf in the back seat. A package of filter cigarettes, and tucked into it a matchfolder from The Pines. That's a motel about fifty miles from here. Maybe the guy spent the last night there."

"You should have been a detective," Jay said admiringly.

"I've thought of it," Monty admitted with a sigh. "In fact, that was my childhood dream. What am I saying? That's been my childhood dream and my adult dream and I guess it will be my dream when I'm an old man. But I never had enough money saved up to put myself in business." He patted his briefcase next to him on the seat. "I just keep living from hand to mouth. I'd like to hang out a shingle: Monty Montague, Detective Service, Limited and Unlimited. Puzzles solved, clues gathered, sorted, identified, and evaluated."

He sighed. "That would be the life for me. No more toothbrushes. Oh well, some day maybe someone will buy a million toothbrushes and then I'll be set. I'd really be Monty Montague, Detective, at your service."

"The license number," Cindy said suddenly. "Did you get the license number?"

Monty slapped his forehead. "A fine detective I'd make," he said sheepishly. "I forgot the most important thing."

"Well, you helped us a lot anyway," Cindy said. "The map and everything. And you helped us escape."

"True, true," Monty said cheerfully. "Now where is this farm I'm supposed to drop you detectives off at?"

"Well," Jay said, "it's not coming up for quite a while." He looked at Cindy. "We didn't even stop to think if it would be out of your way. I hope you don't mind taking us there."

Monty smiled at the Spotlighters through his rear-view mirror. "Well, if it's along this road, there's no problem whatsoever. And if it isn't along this road, it's still not a problem. So how's that? Actually, I'm headed for Kenoska. I've had luck there before."

"Kenoska!" Cindy said. "That's where we live."

"Well, why don't I just drive you home, then? We can talk about unsolved mysteries all the way there," Monty said eagerly.

"We'd love to, but we can't, Monty," Jay said. "There's no way for us to get in touch with the people who are picking us up."

"Right, right, I forgot," Monty said. He turned up the radio a little. "One of my favorite songs," he said to the front window.

Jay and Cindy leaned back in the seat while Monty hummed along with the radio. They had escaped from Scull. They were safe, at least. Now all they had to do was find out whose house in Woodvale was going to be robbed. Or maybe not robbed.

Without the key and combination the Spotlighters had, what could Scull do? Would he call that woman named Jane Jones?

Cindy glanced out the window. Drifts of snow were piled everywhere. There were spots in the road where cars had obviously been stuck earlier. Huge ruts appeared at almost every curve.

Monty drove his car carefully and slowly while the three of them chatted. Before they knew it, the Spotlighters saw a familiar, gnarled tree up ahead on the side of the road.

"The farm house is just at the next bend," Jay said. "It's white, and there's a big brown barn in the yard."

Monty nodded and slowed the car even more. He pulled to a stop in front of a large white farm house. The Fillson's pickup truck was in the driveway.

Monty turned around to face the Spotlighters. "No coats? Is this a survival course, too?"

Cindy nodded quickly. "How did you guess? It's part of learning how to adapt to changing conditions and emergencies."

She saw a shadow of disbelief cross Monty's face. "Anyway, the jackets were pretty old," she added.

"And our family will be picking us up right away," said Jay. "With our new jackets. Otherwise we wouldn't have left the old ones."

"They'll be here any minute," said Cindy. "Thanks a million, Monty."

"Good luck," he said. "Maybe someday I'll read about you in the newspapers, if you decide to be real detectives."

The Spotlighters smiled and got out of the car. "Good luck to you, too, Monty," they called as he pulled away from the side of the road. "Hope someone does buy a million toothbrushes someday." He waved, and the old green car was soon out of sight down the highway.

"I like him," Cindy said. Jay nodded, and they turned from the highway to walk up to the house. The cold wind whipped at their faces.

"Oooh, how I miss my jacket," Cindy moaned, slapping her arms around her.

"Maybe the Fillsons will make us a huge pot of

hot chocolate," Jay said, nearing the large porch of the house.

"I guess they'll be pretty surprised to see us," said Cindy.

"No, Dex said he'd call to let them know," said Jay.

"I'll be glad to get warm," Cindy said. The Spotlighters stamped their feet on the porch, sending slivers of icicles off the railing.

Jay rang the doorbell, jumping from one foot to the other. They stood for a minute. When no one came to the door, he rang the bell again. Cindy looked around the yard. A half-finished snowman stood near the barn, and there were dozens of angels in the snow.

"Maybe they're out behind the barn or something," she suggested. Jay followed her gaze around the yard. Then he stared at the driveway.

"Their truck is here, but their car is gone," he said through chattering teeth. "It looks like they're not here."

Cindy looked at the empty driveway and rubbed her cold arms. "What timing," she said. "We should have called to make sure. Dex probably couldn't reach them, either. And by then we'd left the room so he couldn't call to tell us they weren't home."

"Well, at least Dexter and Anne should be here any minute," Jay said encouragingly. He strained his eyes to look down the highway. All was quiet. Not a car in sight.

"We'd better run around to keep our circulation going," Cindy said, stepping down the porch and into the yard.

"I'm too cold to do any running around," complained Jay. But he stepped off the porch and stomped around the yard.

"We must look ridiculous," he said.

"Who's looking?" asked Cindy, swinging her arms around her in a wide circle. Suddenly she stopped, tilting her head toward a sound from the highway.

"A car!" she announced happily. "Dexter and Anne to the rescue." But in a moment it was clear that the car was coming down the road from the wrong direction.

"The next car, then," Cindy said firmly, and once more stomped around the yard. The faint humming of another car grew louder, and Cindy and Jay watched as it came into view down the highway. It was going pretty fast for such a slippery road. And then it was skimming past the farm house, a bright red car. It suddenly skidded, braking fast.

Cindy sucked in her breath. The car swerved out

of sight beyond the yard. They kept their eyes glued to the highway. And in another moment the red car began backing up over the ice. A large figure was at the wheel.

"Scull!" Cindy screamed. "He's found us!"

7 · Danger in the Barn

CINDY STOOD FROZEN in fear as she stared at the red car. Jay grabbed her arm and pulled her through the snow toward the barn.

"Come on!" he urged hoarsely. "The barn."

"He'll see our footprints," warned Cindy. "He'll know where we're hiding! He'll follow us and—"

"It's our only chance," said Jay. He pulled at her, and she started to run with him, her legs slicing through the deep snow. Frozen pieces of ice cut into her shins, but she felt nothing. She forced her legs to dig through the drifted snow. She did not look over her shoulder.

Jay yanked on the old wooden door, forcing it open. He pulled Cindy in after him and then slammed the door. They breathed the sharp smell of hay.

"Quick!" ordered Jay. "Look for a place to hide." He slid an old wooden bar through the lock and turned to face the barn. There was a hayloft. And stalls. And a small makeshift shed in the far corner.

"The shed," Jay whispered, pointing across the barn. They sped over bits of hay, feeling the cold musty air of the barn settle on them. They reached the small shed, and Jay tugged on the door. It was stuck. He kicked and tried again, opening it at last. The inside was black.

"Get in," he said hoarsely. Cindy stepped into the small shed, feeling her way with her hands. Jay stepped in behind her, pulling the door shut after him. They stood motionless, unable to see anything in the dark, and waited.

Dexter and Anne would be there any minute, Cindy was sure. Before Scull could find them.

Suddenly they heard Scull try the door of the barn. It rattled and creaked. And then he kicked it. After a moment the kicking stopped. There was silence. Cindy blinked her eyes in the blackness of the shed. She grabbed Jay's arm when there was a sudden thumping and crashing against the barn door. And then there was the sound of splintering wood. Scull was breaking into the barn.

Cindy heard herself gasp and had a fleeting memory of Scull's face in the motel closet.

"Shh!" Jay warned.

Scull's inside the barn, Cindy said to herself.

"I know you're in here," came a muffled, angry bellow from somewhere in the barn. "Let's stop playing games. I'll get to you one way or another."

The Spotlighters heard a rustling of dried hay as Scull moved around the barn in the dark. "Rotten kids," he spat. And then the shuffling stopped. There was silence. Cindy hated the silence more than the yelling.

"Hey!" Scull shouted. A laugh bounced off the

barn walls. He's found us, Cindy thought, closing her eyes. He knows we're in the shed.

"The hayloft!" said Scull. They heard a thud and the creaking of wood as Scull began to climb the ladder up to the hayloft.

Hurry, Dexter, Cindy said to herself, her eyes shut tight.

The creaking of the ladder up to the hayloft had stopped, and there was only the muffled sound of footsteps above the Spotlighters.

Suddenly Jay reached over to Cindy and whispered, "The ladder. I could knock the ladder down, and he'd be stuck up there!"

Cindy's eyes widened in the dark. "Yes," she whispered back excitedly.

"You stay here," Jay said. "I'll sneak out and do it."

"No. I'm coming with you," insisted Cindy.

"Okay," Jay said. "Here goes." He reached for the door. It squeaked as it began to swing open. Jay held it, waiting. The footsteps above stopped. Jay's fingers ached to pull the door closed again, but he waited, his heart pounding. The footsteps started moving around again, and Jay pushed the door a bit more. Finally it was open all the way. He stepped quietly out of the shed, pulling Cindy with him. After the pitch blackness of the shed, the barn seemed light. Jay took a deep breath and headed for the ladder. If only he could push it away before Scull knew what was happening.

Before they had gone three feet from the shed, Cindy suddenly pulled hard on Jay's arm. She pointed to the ladder. Scull had already started down. They were too late.

They hurried back to the shed. Jay pulled the door behind them. It squeaked shrilly. His throat went dry.

Scull shouted, "So there you are. Not in the hayloft after all. The shed." They heard his footsteps on the ladder, coming closer.

"Okay. Now I get what belongs to me. And you'll get what's coming to you."

His footsteps stopped right outside the shed door. Jay gripped the handle tightly.

Scull pulled on the door. The handle wrenched from Jay's fingers. The door flew open, and Scull

stood looming above them. His face was ugly and misshapen in the dim light.

"Thought you'd trick me," he said. "Throwing the wrong envelope. Running off. Well, there's no escape now." A cruel smile creased his face. "The girl's had it all along, eh?" He lunged toward Cindy.

"Don't you dare touch her!" Jay shouted, throwing himself between Scull and Cindy.

Scull stood tensed, breathing hard.

"Cindy," Jay whispered hoarsely, "give him everything. Hurry."

Cindy clutched at her pocket and stared at Scull. "You can't have it," she said. Scull looked at her and laughed. "Oh, and a little thing like you is going to stop me, is that what you think?" He moved a step closer to Cindy, his long arm sweeping back threateningly.

"Give it to him," Jay shouted to Cindy.

Cindy's heart pounded. Scull looked at her through slits of eyes, his arm raised. Suddenly she reached into her pocket and grabbed the envelope, thrusting it at Scull. He snatched it from her and quickly searched through it. Satisfied, he jammed the envelope into his own pocket, rocking back on his heels. Then he stared silently down at the Spotlighters.

Cindy felt herself shrinking into the darkness of the shed.

"If my partners knew about you right now, you'd be in even a worse mess. Lucky for you Buzzy has been in hiding lately. But I'm a nice guy. Oh, real nice. I just want you out of my way, right?" He shifted his weight from one foot to the other.

"Get back in there, both of you!" he suddenly shouted. Jay nearly tripped over Cindy as he backed farther into the dark shed. Scull seemed to be talking to himself. "Two kids playing accidentally lock themselves in an old shed." He nodded slowly. Then he slammed the small shed door on Cindy and Jay.

"You'll see," his muffled voice came through the door. Cindy held her breath. She willed herself to keep from screaming.

They heard footsteps and then a loud pounding against the little shed door. Metal against metal.

Scull was nailing them in!

After a moment he stopped. And then his footsteps moved away from them, scuffling through the dried hay.

They heard the big barn door open and then close. They were alone in the barn, nailed in the little shed. Jay stood still, straining his ear against the wood. And then he heard the sound of an engine starting up. It grew loud and then faded away. "He's gone," breathed Cindy.

Jay threw himself against the shed door. It wouldn't budge. He tried again and again, but nothing gave.

"What will we do?" Cindy asked, her voice shaking.

Jay pounded his fists on the door and finally gave up. "Dexter and Anne will be here any minute," he said, out of breath. "And the Fillsons will be coming back. They'll see our tracks in the snow. We're not trapped. As soon as we hear a car in the driveway, we'll start shouting and pounding. We'll be out of here in no time."

Cindy stared in the direction of Jay's voice and said nothing. For the first time since she and Jay had been in the shed, she felt freezing cold. She rubbed her arms furiously and began to stamp up and down.

"Maybe there's an old horse blanket or something in here," Jay said, rummaging around in the dark. He banged his head against something and drew back.

"Who's this Buzzy he mentioned?" Cindy wondered. "His partner? How many are in the gang, anyway? Bee and—" She stopped. "Bee. That wasn't Bee, it was *B*. The initial for Buzzy!"

"And now Scull's on his way to meet Buzzy. They'll rob the safe. There's nothing we can do," said Jay.

"Never give up," Cindy reminded him.

Jay cleared a place for them to sit down. "We'll just have to wait for the Fillsons. Or Dexter and Anne."

"It's so cold," complained Cindy. "It's too dark in here, and we're all alone, and I'm mad and I'm scared."

"Listen!" interrupted Jay.

Cindy strained her ears. She heard a faint ringing. Then it stopped.

"It's the Fillson's phone," Jay said.

"Maybe it's Dexter calling to tell us they can't come," said Cindy. "Maybe they had car trouble, or got stuck in a drift, or—"

"Don't think about it," urged Jay. "Anne and Dexter will be here any minute. It was probably somebody calling for the Fillsons. Anne might be pulling in the driveway right now."

They both listened to the outside sounds but heard nothing. They waited, taking turns rubbing the cold off each other's backs. Cindy began to feel drowsy and longed to lie down. The cold had numbed her fingers so that she could hardly bend them.

"Even my lips are numb," she complained to Jay.

"Mine, too," Jay said. Inside the small dark shed, the noises from outside seemed filtered through thick blankets of snow. Suddenly Jay straightened.

"It's a car," he said softly, trying not to sound too excited. The sound drew nearer and nearer until at last he was sure it was a car pulling into the driveway. They heard the sound of car doors slamming and voices. Cindy nearly wept with relief.

Jay started to pound on the door. Cindy helped, although her hands were so weak she could barely make any noise at all.

"We're in here!" shouted Jay. "Here in the shed in the barn! We're in here!" After a moment he paused and listened. He heard the voices coming closer to the barn. "They heard us!" he said excitedly.

"Come on, Dexter!" Cindy shouted.

"Jay! Cindy!" It was Dexter's voice, then Anne's. "Where are you?"

"Here in the shed!" Jay called. "We've been nailed in!" Dexter and Anne were in the barn running through the hay to the shed.

"Are you all right?" Anne asked, worry catching in her voice.

"We're fine," Cindy answered. "Just cold."

"I'll have you out in a second," Dexter said. He found a hammer in the hay next to the shed and began prying out the large nails from the door. In a moment Dexter pulled the door open. Jay and Cindy tumbled out.

"What happened? What on earth happened?" Anne asked, brushing hay off Cindy's blouse.

"We'll tell you everything when we get in the car," promised Jay. "Just please say the heat's on high."

"Let's go," Dexter said, clapping his hand on Jay's shoulder. They all hurried out of the barn and towards the car.

8 · Hurry!

"BLANKETS ARE in the trunk, Dex," said Anne.

Jay and Cindy sank gratefully into the warm car. Dexter brought the blankets. "We couldn't reach you to say we'd be late," he told them.

"As long as you got here, it's okay," grinned Jay.

"Wow!" said Dexter, pulling his glasses down and turning to Jay and Cindy in the back seat. "Start talking. What's it all about? Who locked you in? Why—"

Jay interrupted. "My teeth are chattering too much to talk. I'll never get warm again."

Cindy took a deep breath. "My teeth are chattering, but not because I'm cold. Being scared stiff is as bad as being frozen stiff."

"And being both is terrible," said Jay.

Anne looked in the rear-view mirror. "You two sure look like something that dropped in from the North Pole. Tell you what. There's a place up here where we can get some hot chili. You can talk while you eat."

"We've got to get to Woodvale," said Cindy.

"I vote for the chili," said Jay. "We both need it. It won't take long."

"But talk 'til we get there," said Dexter. "I'm dying of curiosity."

"Me too," said Anne. "Honestly, anyone who would lock two kids in an empty barn on a day like this—we've got to find out who he is and get the police after him. Oops, here's our chili place. Might as well wait 'til we're inside and sitting in a booth before you start explaining."

In a few minutes they were sitting over four steaming bowls of chili. Jay and Cindy ate quickly as they started to tell Dexter and Anne about their adventures. Cindy took out her notebook.

"Here's what we know," she said. "There's a house in Woodvale. We don't know what house or who lives there. It's got a safe. Scull—the man who locked us in—has one half of the combination. He got it away from us. He's going to meet someone named Buzzy at the house at eight o'clock. Buzzy's got the other half."

"And they each have a key to the house," Jay put in. "One to an outer door and one to an inner door, probably."

Dexter shook his head. His eyes sparkled. "What an adventure!" he said.

"You can say that because you weren't frozen and scared the way we were," said Cindy.

"All we have to figure out is which house it is in Woodvale," said Dexter.

"There are about three thousand houses in Woodvale," said Jay.

"All we can do is go up and down the streets asking if anyone's heard of a dog named Tarrawig," said Cindy.

"There are four of us," said Dexter. "That means if we split up and—"

"We'll each have to cover about six hundred houses," sighed Cindy.

"Tarrawig," said Dexter. "I know I've heard

that name before. But where?" He frowned and pushed his glasses up on his head.

Anne glanced at her watch. "Tell you what. Let's get back in the car and start for Woodvale. A lot of the roads are shut off. The snow's been drifting. I'll do my best to get you there safely and soon and warmly. But we'd better start moving. I've still got to get some gas in the car."

"I think I saw a gas station a little way from here on our way," Dexter said. He turned to Jay and Cindy. "But I still haven't heard everything."

"We'll tell you every single thing from the beginning as soon as we're on our way," promised Cindy. They all got back into the car and in a moment neared the gas station.

Cindy leaned forward, staring ahead. "Hey!" she gasped. "That's Luke's bus!" she said, pointing toward a driveway next to the gas station. "And there's Luke! Cold or not, let's go talk to him, Jay. He must wonder what happened to us."

Anne swung the car up to a gas pump, and Cindy and Jay tumbled out.

"Luke!" Cindy called. "Luke!" Luke turned

around, and his face broke into a broad smile when he saw them.

"I didn't like that one little bit, that you didn't get back on my bus," Luke said sternly, his eyes twinkling. His face grew serious. "Really, you did have me worried."

"We're sorry, Luke," Cindy said. "We just—"

"I know, I know," Luke interrupted, raising a hand up. "Mr. Montague told me your family had come to pick you up. And that was lucky for you," he said with a chuckle. "Here you've been having fun with your family, and all my passengers had to transfer to another bus. Mine's developed some sickly symptoms. Flu, probably."

A mechanic from inside the garage called to him. Luke waved to him and then turned back to Jay and Cindy. "Good luck to you kids," he said. "Hope you ride my line again sometime."

"We will," promised Jay.

Cindy spoke up. "Luke, on the phone this morning you said twenty-four. I was just wondering, what did that mean?"

Luke grinned. "That's the number of my bus,"

he said. "I'd called the bus company to say we were stranded. And they called me back with instructions about paying the motel for all of my passengers." He walked over to the mechanic.

"Oh, good," Cindy said to Jay as they hurried back to Anne's car. "I can cross that off in my notebook."

As soon as they were back in the car, Jay and Cindy started talking again about their adventures. When Cindy got to the part about the man in the closet, she started to shake uncontrollably. "I'm just cold," she said. "It was horrible," she whispered. "Horrible."

Dexter clenched his fists. "Wait 'til we find him, Cindy. We can have him put in jail for locking you and Jay in that barn."

Anne leaned forward, frowning. "Oh, look," she groaned. "Another road blocked off. I've got to take a detour."

"Keep talking," Dexter urged Jay and Cindy. "I've got to know everything."

Cindy and Jay talked quickly, interrupting each other. They told about hiding in Monty's car in their effort to escape Scull, about the map that Monty had seen in Scull's car. "And imagine what we felt like when we were standing in the Fillson's yard watching for you, and Scull drove right by and saw us," said Cindy, shivering.

"And turned around to get us," added Jay.

"What if you hadn't come?" asked Cindy.

Dexter set his jaw. "We'll find him," he promised. "Tell me more."

"I think we've told you everything," said Jay.

"Tell us again," urged Dexter, polishing his glasses. "Maybe you've forgotten one little thing that would be a clue."

Cindy opened her notebook. " 'A. Scull. Jane Jones.' Fake names—they would never use their real names."

"She must be the leader of the gang," said Dexter. "Scull and the other guy, Buzzy, will do the robbery, and then they'll split three ways. No one trusts each other. That's the way it is on TV."

"I'd rather have watched it all on TV than lived through it," sighed Cindy.

"Not me," said Jay firmly.

"What should we do first when we get to Wood-vale?" asked Anne. "Not that we ever will get there, at this rate. Here's another detour. I think we're going in circles."

"When we do get there," said Jay, "we'll just go knocking on doors, asking if anyone knows of a dog named Tarrawig."

"It sounds familiar. But why?" Dexter asked, frowning. "Tarrawig, Tarrawig," he said to himself.

"Maybe he's a show dog," said Jay. "Or one of those racing dogs. You know, the ones that chase a mechanical rabbit."

Dexter shook his head. "It wouldn't have been that kind of thing, or I wouldn't have read about it. Or remembered it."

He closed his eyes. "Tarrawig," he said under his breath. "I know I've heard the name. But it's no use. I can't remember."

"And I can't remember when I've seen so much snow drifting," said Anne. "We're going to have to creep along from here on—look at these ruts! If we go any faster we'll get stuck. Maybe we'll get stuck anyway."

The three Spotlighters peered anxiously ahead at the narrow road.

"What did Scull look like?" asked Dexter.

"Terrible," said Cindy.

"If you'd had a camera you could have taken his picture. Maybe that way the police could have found him," said Dexter.

"You and your camera," laughed Anne. "Honestly, kids, at our cousin's Dex was taking pictures of every single child and every single pet and every single—"

"Pictures of the dogs," said Dexter suddenly. "That's it! That's it! There was an article in the Sunday paper once. About a guy who had photographed his dog from the day it was born right on through. Every single day."

"We've got a mystery to solve," complained Jay. "We haven't got time to talk about photographs."

"The dog's name was Tarrawig!" exploded Dexter.

Cindy and Jay stared. "Are you sure?"

"How could I forget a name like that? And the reason I remember the story is that I thought what a great idea that would be and that I'd do it when I get a dog."

Jay and Cindy sat forward. "But what's the owner's name?" asked Jay.

"I don't remember. I just don't remember."

"Try," urged Cindy. "You remembered the name Tarrawig."

"That's because it was an odd name," said Dexter. "The owner had a regular name. Those are the ones that slip out of your head."

"What about that memory book you were reading?" asked Anne.

Dexter shrugged. "Well, it doesn't always work. I remember his name had something to do with monkeys, that's all. Just the way I'll always remember Scull's name—it has something to do with skulls and bones."

"Okay, his name has something to do with monkeys," said Cindy. "Trees? Swinging? Jungle? Long tails?"

Dexter shook his head.

"Baboon? Chimpanzee? Gorilla? Ape? Orangutan?"

Dexter blinked. "Gibbon," he said. "Jeremiah Gibbon."

They all drew a sharp breath. "We've got it," Jay shouted, pounding Dexter on the back.

Dexter grinned from ear to ear. "Hey, I guess that memory book didn't turn out to be such a dumb idea after all."

"Now all we have to do is get to Woodvale and look his address up in a phone book," said Cindy. She glanced at her watch. "We have just enough time to beat them there."

They all faced ahead. Anne hunched over the steering wheel. "We'll make it," she promised. "We'll make it."

"Please let us be in time," said Cindy under her breath.

"Then we'll look up Jeremiah Gibbon's name in the phone book," said Jay.

"If we get there," worried Cindy.

"Think positive," said Dexter.

Just then Anne spun the wheel of the car around to avoid a drift, and the car skidded, sliding across the road. In another moment it lurched into a drift, and the wheels spun uselessly. Anne put the car in reverse. It wouldn't move.

"Oh, no," groaned Dexter.

"Let me try again," Anne said, throwing the car in gear and accelerating. A high-pitched whine came from the spinning wheels. Jay looked out the back window and saw spurts of snow flying up.

"It's no use," Anne said. "We'll have to push. If you three can rock it, I'll try to get it out."

The three Spotlighters jumped out of the car, Cindy and Jay wrapped in blankets. Jay peered down at the wheel that was stuck. It was buried inches deep in an icy rut. "Let's all get behind," he called. In a moment, they were shoving and pushing while the wheels spun madly.

"It's already six-thirty," Dexter groaned. "We're late as it is without this mess." He shook his head and the Spotlighters stood back from the car. "We'll have to get something under that wheel. Some branches, maybe."

Hurriedly the Spotlighters gathered some branches together and stuffed them in the rut.

"Try it now, Anne," Dexter called. The three

pushed again. The car started clearing the rut as bits of branches flew from behind the wheel.

"Harder!" grunted Jay. In a burst the car was freed, and they hurried back into the warmth.

Had they lost too much time?

Would they be too late?

9 · Mr. Gibbon's Visitors

ANNE DROVE CAREFULLY and slowly during the next hour while the Spotlighters huddled, silent, in their seats. The headlights stabbed the dark road ahead, showing glimpses of snow-laden trees.

As they rounded a bend in the road, the headlights picked up a snowy sign, its lettering barely legible.

"Woodvale!" Cindy said excitedly. "Eight miles!"

Dexter peered at his watch in the dark of the car. "It's 7:30. If we can get to a phone booth in Woodvale in fifteen minutes and look up Mr. Gibbon's address, we just might make it."

"We'll make it," Anne said, pushing the accelerator down gently. The Spotlighters were quiet as the car made its way through the still, winding streets leading to Woodvale.

In ten minutes Anne slowed the car. "There!" she said. "A phone booth." She pulled the car next to it, and Dexter jumped out.

"Gibbon, Gibbon, Gibbon," he muttered to himself as he flipped through the phone book. He ran a smudged finger down the pages. "Here! Gibbon, Jeremiah, 13 Hillcrest Lane." He quickly memorized the address and slammed the book shut.

"Thirteen Hillcrest Lane," he said breathlessly as he jumped back in the car.

Anne stared at the road ahead of her. Huge white drifts of snow bowed down the trees. "I haven't the faintest notion where Hillcrest Lane is," she said miserably. "And we've got only twenty minutes!"

"Wait!" demanded Dexter. He leaped out of the

car again and was back in a second, holding the Woodvale phone book in his hand. "We can return it later. It's got a map in the front." He opened the book. "Okay, make a left up at the next corner and keep going until Ridge Road."

Anne nodded and pulled the car away from the side of the road. In a moment they had reached the corner and found Ridge Road. "Hillcrest Lane should be about six blocks from here," Dexter said excitedly.

The Spotlighters peered ahead. "Just look at the houses!" Cindy exclaimed, her eyes wide. Enormous white lawns spread out in front of the huge mansions.

"Here's Hillcrest Road," Anne said. The car slowly wound through the narrow road. Snow-covered trees arched above them.

"See if you can catch any numbers," Anne said. Dexter, Jay, and Cindy strained their eyes toward the houses.

"Nothing," Jay said, worry in his voice.

"Wait a minute," Dexter said, blinking his eyes behind his glasses. "There's a number on that post over there," he said, pointing to a small sign at the side of the road. "Let me check." He jumped out of the car, and Jay and Cindy watched as he brushed off the sign. A large "23 Hillcrest" stared back at them.

Dexter hurried back. "All we have to do is find the right sign," he said.

Anne moved the car again, slowly, to each of the next posts. In a few minutes they had found the one that read "13 Hillcrest."

"This is it!" Jay said. He looked around at the winding road and the long path that led up to the house. Huge trees lined the walk.

"We can't park here," Dexter said, frowning. "Scull and Buzzy will be along, and they'll see the car. Let's move it down the road and park it in one of those out-of-the-way lanes we saw."

Anne nodded and turned the car carefully around. In a few moments the four stepped out, Jay and Cindy hugging their blankets to them. Quickly they made their plans.

"Let's see if we can get around the back way somehow," Jay whispered. "If we go up that long front walk, Scull might see us. He should be getting here any minute."

Cindy shivered. She didn't think it was from the cold. Wordlessly, the three Spotlighters and Anne started walking towards Mr. Gibbon's house. The snow crunched beneath their feet. They found a narrow path that skirted the houses in the back. It looked as though it had been shoveled recently. The trees in the dim moonlight cast eerie shadows across the lawns. Were they all tree shadows, Cindy wondered. What if Scull were somewhere near, hiding?

Suddenly the Spotlighters heard a soft thud behind them. Cindy whirled around, her throat dry, afraid to look. Scull? Had he seen them and followed them after all?

Jay laughed nervously. "Just snow falling off the trees," he whispered, pointing to the ground behind them where a fresh pile of snow had landed on the shoveled path. Cindy wrapped the blanket more tightly around her.

They were nearing the house.

"It's a quarter to eight," Dexter whispered urgently. "We've got no time to lose. Scull could be sneaking up the front walk this very minute."

Cindy closed her eyes against the chilly wind,

but she did not feel cold anymore. Her face was burning.

"Now let's sneak around to the front," Jay suggested. They slowly made their way around the house, the snow beneath them crunching softly. They turned a corner and there it stood. A huge front door, firmly closed against the night. Tall bushes lined the front porch, sagging beneath the weight of snow.

"You all stay hidden," suggested Dexter. "Scull doesn't know me. I'll ring the doorbell. If he sees me he'll think I'm the paper boy, collecting." He crossed his fingers and took a deep breath.

"Take care," whispered Cindy.

As he pressed the doorbell, Dexter could hear the muffled chime echoing through the rooms of the big house.

There was silence. Just as Dexter reached to push the doorbell once again, a bolt was pushed and the door opened. A young man with a round flushed face stood in the doorway. He was wearing an overcoat.

"Mr. Gibbon?" asked Dexter.

The young man shook his head. "Mr. Gibbon

cannot see anyone," he said firmly. He started to close the door.

"It's terribly important," said Dexter urgently.

"Sorry about that," muttered the round-faced young man. "We're leaving for the airport. Mr. Gibbon has a plane to catch."

Dexter thought quickly. That's why the thieves would have an hour. This man was taking Mr. Gibbon to the airport.

The door started to close. Quickly Dexter pushed it open farther, throwing the young man a little off balance. Flushing, he drew himself up. Dexter realized he way going to hit him. He probably thought Dexter was forcing himself into the house to hold them up or something.

"Wait, you've got to listen!" It was Jay. Suddenly the others were on the doorstep, and just as suddenly they were all inside the house facing a sputtering young man with a red face.

Jay closed the door so if Scull came, he wouldn't see them all standing on the threshhold. The man looked angrily from one to the other. Then he relaxed a little. With two of them wrapped in blankets, these youngsters obviously were not a gang of thugs.

"There's no time to lose," said Dexter urgently. "We've got to set a trap. Someone is coming to rob Mr. Gibbon's safe."

A stair creaked, and Cindy glanced behind Dexter. A slender old man with white hair and a trim white beard was walking down the wide stairway in the hall.

"Mr. Gibbon," said Cindy in a loud voice, and everyone turned to see him.

"Look here," he said. "I don't care what you are selling or what good cause you represent. I don't have time to listen, I don't have time to contribute. My secretary and I are just leaving for the airport. Doug, see these youngsters out. And if you'll be kind enough to bring my suitcase down to the car—"

Jay stood in front of Mr. Jeremiah Gibbon. "Mr. Gibbon, please! We're here because we know someone is coming to rob your safe tonight."

"Who, pray?" asked Mr. Gibbon calmly.

"We don't know their real names," Jay admitted.

"But we know they're coming," Dexter added.

"Indeed," said Mr. Gibbon.

"Really, Mr. Gibbon, you've got to believe us," insisted Cindy.

Mr. Gibbon raised his hands, palms up. "Oh my, I think you young people have let your imaginations run away with you." He smiled a thin smile. "It's all right. I used to play detective myself when I was your age. Keeps the juices flowing."

"But we're not *playing* detectives, we *are* detectives," said Cindy. "And—"

Mr. Gibbon sighed. "I will miss my plane. You'll excuse me, please. Doug, I'll meet you at the car. Good night, young ladies, young men. I don't mean to be rude, but I must ask you to leave now so that I will make my plane connections." He turned to go.

"Mr. Gibbon!" Cindy stepped forward. "Your dog, Tarrawig. He's been poisoned, hasn't he?"

"Poisoned?" Mr. Gibbon's voice raised in dismay. "No, he—"

The young man named Doug interrupted. "Tarrawig had a slight indisposition. He is being treated at the vets. But—poisoned?" He shook his head and glanced at Jeremiah Gibbon.

Cindy sighed in relief. "Thank heaven he's all right. But someone did try to poison him. That's why he's sick."

"The ones who tried to poison Tarrawig, they're the thieves," said Jay. "They're coming in a few minutes. We want to set a trap for them."

"We want you to be here hiding when they come, Mr. Gibbon," said Dexter. "And then the police—"

"Police? Really. I'm not going to be made a laughingstock. Just because my dog is ill—" He glanced at his watch. "We must hurry, Doug."

Cindy opened her notebook. "Mr. Gibbon, is this the last part of your safe combination?"

He stared at the notebook and then at Cindy. He turned to Doug.

"Not even you know this combination," he said in a low controlled voice. "How could anyone find out?"

Doug shook his head dazedly. "It's impossible," he said. "Impossible."

"It's the way I've always told you, Doug," Mr. Gibbon said. "We need a good private detective agency in this area. The police already have their hands full."

Dexter spoke up. "Mr. Gibbon, we must act quickly. Now you believe us. There isn't even time to call the police. The thieves would see them. They'd run away and would never be found. And nothing could ever be proved. We have to set a trap."

Jeremiah Gibbon rubbed his forehead. "Of course," he said. "Doug, we will do as they say." He spoke firmly now. "What do you suggest?"

"They will be here in a few minutes," said Jay. "They will wait and watch for you and Doug to leave. They'll see you leaving—but you will still be here."

Dexter spoke up. "What he means is that Anne, my sister, will wear your coat and hat. She's your height. She will leave with Doug and the suitcases. They won't be expecting disguises so they won't look too closely."

"So they'll think that Doug and I are leaving for the airport," said Jeremiah Gibbon.

"Yes," said Anne. "And we'll call the police as soon as we find a telephone out of sight."

"They know the coast will be clear," said Dexter. "They think Tarrawig has been poisoned. Luckily, the poison only made him sick."

"They believe they have one hour," said Cindy. "As soon as the car leaves they will come in. And we'll be hiding."

She shut her eyes for a moment to try to picture the diagram. "There's a dressing room right off the master bedroom where the safe is," she said. "We could hide there and wait for them."

"And we'll have the police here in time to surprise them," said Anne.

Jeremiah Gibbon took a deep breath. "Very well. We'll do it. Doug, will you please bring my suitcases down and take them and the young lady to the car."

He walked to a closet and took out a coat and a hat. "Here, young lady. Put these on. If you pull the coat collar up and keep your chin down, no one will notice that you have no beard."

By the time Anne had put the hat and coat on, Doug had arrived downstairs with the suitcases. "If you will please follow me," said Doug, his face even redder than before.

Anne followed him out the back way to the garage. "We'll call the police as soon as we are sure we're out of sight," she promised. "And as soon as we find a telephone."

"Now," said Mr. Gibbon, turning to the three Spotlighters. "To our hiding place."

10 · Waiting

IT WAS ONLY when Jeremiah Gibbon led the way up the curving staircase that Cindy noticed the many photographs on the wall. A beautiful collie at different stages, in different settings. Tarrawig.

The same stair creaked as they stepped on it. The three Spotlighters followed Jeremiah Gibbon into a large bedroom. Cindy's eyes were wide. She had never seen a bedroom like this before. It was twice as big as their living room at home. A desk, comfortable chairs, bookshelves, and tables. And a bed. Photographs of the same beautiful collie lined the walls.

Jeremiah Gibbon walked over to one of the tables. "This is the safe," he said. "It looks like a table, but it isn't."

Off the bedroom was a smaller room lined with closets. As soon as they were all inside the room, Mr. Gibbon closed the door and turned off the light. "I'm afraid you'll have to sit on the floor if you want to sit down," he said.

"I'm too excited to sit down," said Cindy. "But I'm too tired to stand up."

They sat on the floor, holding their breath. The minutes passed. Where was Scull, anyway? Maybe he hadn't met Buzzy. Maybe—

They all heard it at the same time. The sound of a door downstairs being opened.

Scull had arrived.

They waited breathlessly, then they heard a muffled voice. "Let's make this quick, Buzzy."

It was Scull's voice. Cindy would have recognized it anywhere.

The man called Buzzy made a grunting noise, and then there were stealthy footsteps on the stairs. The one stair creaked, then creaked again. Cindy felt Mr. Gibbon suck in his breath. He stood perfectly still.

Scull and Buzzy inched their way up the stairs.

Their footsteps were separated by long seconds, and finally Cindy heard them reach the top of the landing.

"In here," Scull said in a low voice.

Cindy heard them enter the bedroom. They couldn't have been more than ten feet from their hiding place. The two men did not speak, and they seemed to be standing in one spot. Cindy could only hear a slight muffled noise. What were they doing? Were they working on the combination of the safe? Or had they heard them, hiding in the dressing room? Did they have guns?

Then a hurried, low voice interrupted the silence. "Right 67, left 13. And that's it!" Scull said in a high whisper. "That's the ball game! We've done it."

"Easy now," said Buzzy. "Here, I'll hold the bag. You put the stuff in."

Cindy felt Jeremiah Gibbon stiffen beside her. His hand reached for the doorknob. Then he hesitated and drew it away. He's waiting until the police come, thought Cindy. But what if they didn't come in time? The Spotlighters and Mr. Gibbon would have to face Scull and the other man. She swallowed.

Then suddenly she heard it: car doors slamming, footsteps. Scull's voice uttering a single strangled oath. Then he whispered hoarsely, "Quick. Someone's here. Maybe Gibbon and that man secretary have come back. We can deal with them. Let's get the stuff in the bag first."

Footsteps. Then a voice, over a megaphone, coming in loud. "Okay, this is the police. Come out with your hands up. No monkey business. This is the police."

Scull uttered another strangled oath. His voice was frantic. "Let's run for it. There must be another way out."

Suddenly the door of the dressing room was flung open. Scull stood there, holding a suitcase, his jaw dropping in shock, his eyes widening in disbelief as he saw them standing there. Behind him stood a small man in a stocking mask—Buzzy. As Scull saw Jeremiah Gibbon and the Spotlighters, he turned to run. The police barred the way.

The Spotlighters would never forget the next few moments. Soon Scull and his partner, handcuffed, walked down the stairs ahead of the police.

"Before you take them away," said Dexter firmly, "can't they answer some questions?"

"Sorry," said a policeman, "But we've got to tell them they have a right to remain silent until they have the advice of counsel."

"Forget that part," snarled Buzzy. "We know what our rights are. It's not the first time around for us. But we want to talk, right, Scull? And we want to talk right here and right now."

Scull scowled and nodded. "We've got nothing to lose anymore," he said.

Buzzy nodded. "We took the stuff, yeah, sure, but who thought of it, huh? Who put us up to it? And she promised there wouldn't be a hitch."

Scull glared at him and then turned to glare at Cindy and Jay. His lip curled in hatred.

Buzzy went on in a whiny voice. "She put us up to it, all right. She planned the whole thing. Told us we'd be home free. We would have gone straight, honest, but she talked us into it. Said it would be a cinch."

"Buzzy's right," Scull said. "We were out on parole. She was on the Rehabilitation Board. The do-gooders who try to get us jailbirds back on the right track."

"Yeah," said Buzzy gloomily. "She set this all up. We were to do the job and bring her the money. She would give us phony passports and some money so we could fly out of this country and be free for good."

"Free and rich," said Scull. He scowled at Cindy and Jay.

"Otherwise I'da gone straight for good, honest," whined Buzzy.

Jeremiah Gibbon stepped forward. "Who is she? And how did she get the combination of my safe? How did she know the layout of my home? How—"

Scull shrugged. "Beats me. We figured she was a good friend of yours. The name she gave us was Jane Jones. We figured it was a phony, of course."

"But who is she, really? I know no one of that name. What did she look like?" asked Mr. Gibbon.

Scull leaned forward, his head lowered. "She looked sharp. Bright. She looked like a winner. Brown hair pulled back in a barrette. Big glasses.

Nose turned up. Mouth turned down. Young, kind of." He drew back. "She's in it with us. More than in it. Like Buzzy says, it was her idea. We go to jail, she goes."

"But I don't know who it can be," repeated Mr. Gibbon.

"She knows you," said Buzzy. "She said she knew you real well." He tilted his head and looked at the ceiling. "Called you Jerry Mia."

Jeremiah Gibbon stared. "Jerry Mia! That's my doctor," he said slowly. "That's Dr. Tiffany Morgan. She's the only one who ever called me that." His face whitened.

"That figures," said Scull. "Maybe she made a house call once, twice, maybe when you were sick, maybe she picked up your wallet, maybe in your wallet you keep the combination of the safe, maybe the keys, maybe—"

Mr. Gibbon put his hand up. "Enough. That's just what happened. I was sick last spring. She did come. That's when she must have looked through my wallet and found the combination and the keys." He turned to the policemen. "Dr. Tiffany Morgan, 33

Skinner Row, Apartment 6. It all fits in. I remember now—she was doing something connected with the prison reform thing. One of her good deeds." His mouth turned down in disgust.

The policeman nodded. Then he turned to Scull and Buzzy. "Okay, you guys. You come with me."

"But you're going to get this Jane Jones? This Dr. Tiffany Morgan?"

"She goes with us," said the policeman. "Don't worry about that."

In a little while the three Spotlighters and Anne sat in Jeremiah Gibbon's living room, sipping hot cocoa.

"What can I ever do to repay you?" asked Jeremiah Gibbon, looking from one to the other.

They glanced at each other.

"Nothing," said Dexter. "We just like to solve mysteries."

"And prevent crimes," added Cindy.

"But I'd like to do something," insisted Jeremiah Gibbon.

Jay shook his head. "No, there's nothing, Mr. Gibbon," he said.

Cindy cleared her throat. "You said there should be a good private detective agency around here," she said.

Mr. Gibbon raised his eyebrows.

"We know a very good detective, as a matter of fact," said Jay, reaching into his pocket. He drew out Monty Montague's calling card and handed it to Jeremiah Gibbon.

"Monty Montague, eh? If you all say he's good, I'll take your word for it," said Mr. Gibbon. "I'll talk to him about starting his own detective agency right away. How's that for a beginning?"

Cindy sighed happily. "For a beginning, that makes a perfect ending," she said.